To Simmo, Marie,
Laura & James

...e w...
about chocolate:

"Why do Easter eggs always run out?"
Daisy

"Do hamsters eat carpet?"
Gabby

"Tweet, tweet, tweet!"
An Easter chick

"Baaaaaaaaaaaaaaaaaaaaaaaaa!"
An Easter Lamb

"I've been robbed!"
The Easter Bunny

"Nooo, Daisy,
noooooooooooooooo!!!!!!"
Daisy's mum

www.penguin.co.uk/ladybird

More Daisy adventures!

DAISY

and the TROUBLE with
CHOCOLATE

by Kes Gray

RED FOX

RED FOX

UK I USA I Canada I Ireland I Australia
India I New Zealand I South Africa

Red Fox is part of the Penguin Random House group of companies whose addresses
can be found at global.penguinrandomhouse.com.

www.penguin.co.uk
www.puffin.co.uk
www.ladybird.co.uk

Penguin
Random House
UK

First published 2017

003

Text copyright © Kes Gray, 2017
Cover illustration © Nick Sharratt, 2017
Interior illustrations copyright © Garry Parsons, 2017
Character concept copyright © Kes Gray, 2017

The moral right of the author and illustrators has been asserted.

Set in VAG Rounded Light 15pt/23pt
Printed in Great Britain by Clays Ltd, St Ives plc

A CIP catalogue record for this book is available from the British Library.

ISBN: 978-1-782-95609-9

Penguin Random House is committed to a sustainable future
for our business, our readers and our planet. This book is
made from Forest Stewardship Council® certified paper.

MIX
Paper from
responsible sources
FSC
www.fsc.org
FSC® C018179

CHAPTER 1

The **trouble with chocolate** is chocolate! If chocolate wasn't so chocolaty, I would never have got into so much trouble over Easter.

I mean, why do people even do chocolate Easter eggs at Easter? Before Easter comes along I am quite happy eating strawberry Dip Dab lollies and Crunchy Cream biscuits.

Neither of those has got even the teensiest bit of chocolate in them at all. They don't even say "chocolate" on the wrapper.

If you ask me, the more people *make* chocolate, the more children will want to *eat* chocolate. Especially at Easter, and double especially if they let children into the place where chocolate is actually made. The places where chocolate is made should be absolutely closed to children if you ask me. But they're not. They are wide open, especially if your mum has a special Easter voucher to go to Chocolate Land. And triple especially if your neighbour knows someone who actually works there. WHICH ISN'T MY FAULT!

CHAPTER 2

I wasn't even thinking about chocolate when my school broke up for the Easter holidays. All I was thinking about was Pickle and Pops. Pickle and Pops are our class hamsters. They've been living in our classroom since half term.

When Mrs Peters told us we were getting real live hamsters to live in our classroom, I nearly fell off my chair I was so excited!

As soon as she brought them in to show us, I asked if they could

live in my desk. But she said no. Mrs Peters said that school desks were really no places for hamsters – which isn't true because my desk is full of places that hamsters would really like, especially inside my pencil case. (Once I'd emptied out my pencils and pens.)

Mrs Peters said that pencil cases were made for pencils and pens to live in, not hamsters, and that if I rolled my exercise books into tunnels, I would spend an extra hour after school flattening the pages out again.

So the hamsters have to live on top of the stationery cupboard instead.

The **trouble with stationery cupboards** is the one in our class is right at the back of the room.

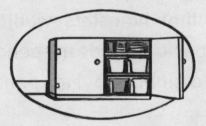

Which means if I want to see what Pickle and Pops are doing, I need to turn my head all the way round. And even then it's not that easy to

see inside their cage, because Tamsin Chance and Letitia Sparks' heads are always in the way.

Tamsin Chance and Letitia Sparks are the luckiest children in our class because their desk is closest to the hamster cage. They still have to turn their heads round to see them, though.

The **trouble with turning your head round in class** is Mrs Peters doesn't like it. Especially if she is teaching you lessons at the same time.

During lessons, Mrs Peters says everyone has to face the whiteboard, not the hamsters, which is silly really because hamsters are far more interesting than lessons.

When I asked if the hamster cage could go by the whiteboard, Mrs Peters said no – plus, if I said one more word about hamsters or cages, then I could go by the whiteboard myself. So I don't really turn my head round in class any more. Unless Jack Beechwhistle is pinging rubber bands at me. Or it's my turn to be Hamster Guardian of the Day.

Every day during term time, we take it in turns to be Hamster Guardian of the Day. Hamster Guardian of the Day day is the day I look forward to most because it means you are totally in charge of Pickle and Pops from the moment the school bell rings in the morning to the moment you have to go home.

It's so brilliant! The moment Mrs Peters has finished calling the register you get to feed them! Plus, if your turn comes on a Friday, you get to clean out their cage too!

The **trouble with feeding hamsters** is you can't just give them any old food – you have to give them exactly the right things. Otherwise they'll turn into guinea pigs.

Every day Pickle and Pops need fresh water in their water bottle, plus a tablespoon of normal hamster food each, plus a piece of fruit (Pickle likes apple, Pops prefers blueberries). Or if there isn't any fruit, you can give them something like carrot, cauliflower or green beans. But don't cook them – they prefer them raw.

The **trouble with cleaning out Pickle and Pops's cage** is you have to wait till lunch-time break to do it because cleaning takes loads more time than feeding, especially the way I do it.

If I had to choose between feeding Pickle and Pops and cleaning them out, I'd choose cleaning them out because then I get to count how many poos they've done in a week.

Hamster poos are really cute and really tiny (about the size of a fairy poo, I reckon). Plus hamsters do loads! The most hamster poos I've counted in one week is 707. The second most is 697. Barry Morely has done the sums for me and says that, on average, Pickle and Pops do over fifty poos a day. EACH! How amazing is that? Imagine going to the loo fifty times a day. Imagine how many loo rolls you would need! And how many lessons you would miss . . .

Hamsters don't use loo rolls, by the way. They just do their business on the floor, in the sawdust. They even poo in their bed!

I'd never poo in my bed. Not unless I'd eaten a half-sucked strawberry Dip Dab I'd picked up off the road that was covered in germs. But that's a different story.

When Mrs Peters asked me if I would like to be Hamster Guardian of the Easter Holiday, I couldn't believe my ears. Me, Daisy Butters, the first ever person in our class to get to look after Pickle and Pops at home!!!!

I don't think Pickle and Pops could believe their ears either because when I looked at their cage, BOTH of them were wide awake. (I don't know if you know, but hamsters do loads of sleeping during the day, so they MUST have been really pleased to hear that they would be going home with me.)

I think Mrs Peters chose me because I am always volunteering to do extra hamster work during break time and after school. Plus she knows I don't have an actual pet of my own at home.

When I told Gabby, I thought she might be a bit jealous, but Gabby has a pet cat called Satan at home.

The **trouble with pet cats called Satan** is they eat hamsters, or at least they would if they got a chance,

so there is no way she would want to look after Pickle and Pops at home.

I did, though! All I had to do was persuade my mum.

CHAPTER 3

As soon as the bell for morning break went that Wednesday, Gabby and me ran out into the playground to read the special letter that Mrs Peters had given me to take home to my mum. It said:

Dear Mrs Butters,

As part of a new and exciting initiative to increase your child's awareness of the natural world, our class has welcomed two hamsters into its fold. Pickle and Pops are firm favourites with the children, but will be looking for a home outside of school for the duration of the Easter holidays. Can you help? Would you and your child be willing and able to look after two lovable hamsters, returning them safely to the school after the holiday?

If so, please tick each of the boxes below accordingly, sign and return to the school office.

☐ Yes, my child and I would be delighted to look after Pickle and Pops!

☐ My child and I have no known allergy to hamsters.

☐ My child and I have no known allergy to standard hamster food or sawdust.

☐ My child and I have no known allergy to fruit or vegetables.

I/We accept full responsibility for any discomfort that may occur as a direct or indirect result of lifting a hamster cage. ☐

I/We accept full responsibility for any disorientation, dizziness and/or any other side effects that may be caused by the repetitive spinning of a hamster's wheel.* ☐

Signature of Parent……………………........................

*And undertake to pay for any veterinary attention that may be needed over the said period of hamster care.

It took me and Gabby nearly the whole of morning break to read the letter. We understood the "Dear Mrs Butters" bit, but got really confused by all the rest.

"What if your mum gets confused too?" asked Gabby. "What if she gets so confused by the letter she won't sign the form?"

"I'm going to put ticks in all the boxes and sign it for her," I said, getting my pencil case out of my school bag.

The **trouble with filling in a form for your mum** is you have to make it look like your mum has done all the filling in.

Trouble is, I did it in purple felt-tip. When I showed my filled-in form to Gabby, she said that parents don't usually write in purple felt-tip, plus they usually do joined-up writing, plus I had signed "Mum" instead of Tiffany Butters.

Which meant there was no way Mrs Peters would believe my mum had filled in the form.

Which meant there was no way Mrs Peters would believe my mum had said yes.

Which meant there was no way I could give the form back to Mrs Peters.

Which meant I had to screw it up into a ball and throw it in the rubbish bin.

Which meant I DIDN'T EVEN HAVE

A SPECIAL LETTER TO TAKE HOME ANY MORE!

The **trouble with not having a special letter to take home any more** is, I had to persuade Mrs Peters to give me another one.

"Say a dog ate it," said Gabby.

"There aren't any dogs in the playground," I said.

"Say Jack Beechwhistle ate it," said Gabby.

"It's OK," I said. "I know exactly

what I'm going to tell her."

The **trouble with telling Mrs Peters that the wind had blown the letter out of my hand during morning break and a bird had swooped down and carried it off in its beak** is, I'm not sure she believed me at first.

"I never knew we had pelicans in the area, Daisy," she said. "Or perhaps it was a toucan?"

"I'm not sure," I said, "but its beak was massive! In fact, I was lucky it didn't fly off with my school bag as well!"

Luckily Mrs Peters totally believed me and gave me another letter to take home.

Only this time I didn't fill it in.

This time I decided to cross my fingers instead.

CHAPTER 4

When I ran out after school to meet my mum, I was so excited I could have burst. Thank goodness I'd been to the loo – because guess what? MY MUM SAID YES! As long as it would be *me* looking after the hamsters over the holiday and not *her*. Which was a bit of a weird thing to say, if you ask me.

Gabby was really excited for me too, especially when my mum said I could keep Pickle and Pops in my bedroom. Mum even said I could

put their cage right beside my bed. I couldn't believe it! It was going to be the best Easter holiday EVER!!!!!!!!

I didn't care whose turn it was to feed Pickle and Pops for the rest of the week now, or even who got to clean them out, because I knew that as soon as we broke up from school on Friday I was going to have Pickle and Pops ALL to myself for a whole TWO WEEKS!

And their cage! And their wheel! And their food! And their drinks bottle! And their sawdust! And everything!

I would be able to feed them every day and even clean them out every day if I wanted to!

How brilliant is that!?

All I had to do now was wait to take them home.

And wait.

And wait.

And wait.

And wait.

The **trouble with being told on a Wednesday that you are going to be Hamster Guardian of the Easter Holiday** is, once Wednesday's over, you still have to wait for Thursday to be over before you even get to Friday.

Plus, even when you get to Friday, you have to do another whole day of lessons before you break up for the Easter holidays at the end of the afternoon.

It was soooooooo frustrating.

My mum told me that I should stop wishing my life away, but I wasn't wishing my life away at all, I was just wishing my life had real live actual hamsters in it, living with me at home. Why did I have to go to boring school first?

Why couldn't I be Hamster Guardian of the Easter Holiday straight away?!

I don't know how many rubber bands Jack Beechwhistle pinged at me over the last two days of school, but he was definitely, definitely jealous.

In the playground on Thursday, Jack told me and Gabby that about five hundred years ago a really bad disease called the Great Plague of London had been caused by hamsters and that I would probably catch it too now. Luckily Barry Morely was listening, so when Jack had gone, he told us it wasn't caused by hamsters at all. It was caused by rats, which don't even look anything like hamsters because they have much longer tails.

When I asked my mum, she said the Great Plague of London wasn't even caused by rats. It was caused

by fleas that lived on rats. Which was even better news because fleas don't look anything like hamsters either, and even if they did, Pickle and Pops don't have any fleas, because if they did, I would have noticed them when I was being hamster monitor. So there was no way I was going to catch the Great Plague of London. Or even the Little Plague of London. And even if I did, the first thing I would do when I got back to school is breathe it all over Jack Beechwhistle. That would stop him and his rubber bands.

When the bell fiiiiiiiiiiiiiiiiiiiinally

went at the end of school on Friday, it felt like I'd been waiting about twenty weeks!

And even then I had to wait for my mum to turn up!

And wait and wait and wait.

Because when she did turn up and saw me and Gabby by the hamsters, she had to go all the way home again because she had forgotten to bring the car with her! It was soooooo embarrassing.

When my mum finally turned up and Mrs Peters finally gave me Pickle and Pops's cage to hold, I was so excited I nearly burst. Mum took the hamster food and Gabby carried the sawdust. We had absolutely everything we needed for the perfect holiday.

"Happy Easter!" said Mrs Peters as we left the classroom.

"You too," said my mum. "See you in two weeks!"

I'd never carried a hamster cage out of a classroom before. It was so brilliant! When we got to the car, Mum made me give her the cage to hold while Gabby and I got in and did up our seat belts. But as soon as my seat belt was clicked I made Mum give me the cage back straight away.

"They've woken up!" said Gabby, poking her finger through the bars.

Gabby was right – Pickle and Pops definitely looked more jumpity than before.

"I think they are excited about coming to live with me!" I said.

"I'D BE EXCITED ABOUT COMING TO LIVE WITH YOU!" said Gabby as we pulled up outside her house. "ESPECIALLY FOR TWO WEEKS!"

"I know!" I grinned. "If next Friday is called Good Friday, then this Friday should be called Best Friday!"

"Best EVER Friday!" Gabby waved. "See you tomorrow!"

When we arrived at my house, I couldn't get my seat belt off quick enough. As soon as I got Pickle and Pops through the front door, I carried them straight up to my bedroom. Mum helped with the sawdust and food, but I was totally in charge of their cage.

"I wonder if they eat Easter eggs," I said as I settled them down on the table next to my bed.

"NO, THEY DO NOT EAT EASTER EGGS!" growled my mum. "Chocolate was not designed for hamsters,

Daisy. In fact, it is one of the worst things you can ever feed an animal."

"I was only wondering," I said. "I wasn't going to actually give them any."

"I'm pleased to hear it," Mum frowned.

"I wonder if they are hungry, though," I said, lying down on my bed and watching them from my pillow.

"They have plenty of food to eat if they are," said Mum.

"I wonder if they are thirsty," I said.

"They know where their water bottle is if they are," said Mum.

"I wonder if they fancy some fruit," I said.

"There is fruit in the fruit bowl if they do," said Mum.

"I wonder if their whiskers need brushing," I said.

"You can keep your hands off my hairbrush if they do," said Mum.

"I wonder if their wheel needs oiling," I said.

"You can stay out of the shed if it does," said Mum.

"I wonder if their toenails need clipping," I said.

"Not even with the red scissors," Mum frowned.

"I wonder if they want me to read them a story," I said.

"I wonder if this is going to be the longest two weeks of my life," sighed my mum. "Oh good, there's someone at the door!"

CHAPTER 5

I was far too busy thinking about Pickle and Pops to even notice our doorbell. It was our neighbour Mrs Pike. She had seen me arrive home from school and had something she wanted to give to my mum.

And to me.

"Best Ever Friday just got even better, Daisy!" said Mum, coming back into my bedroom waving two pieces of paper. "Look! Two FREE tickets to the Spirit of Easter Festival at Chocolate Land!"

"CHOCOLATE LAND!" I gasped. "FREE!!!???" I spluttered.

"A free ticket for you and a free ticket for me!" Mum smiled. "All thanks to our lovely neighbour Mrs Pike, whose brother just happens to work there!"

I couldn't believe it! Not only did I have two cute, adorable hamsters called Pickle and Pops in my house, we now had two tickets to one of the best places in the whole entire world to get excited about too.

FOR FREE!!

The **trouble with cuddling hamsters too tight** is their eyeballs will pop out.

So I decided to give Mum a big hug instead.

Once I'd finished my hug, and once I'd absolutely totally made definitely sure that Pickle and Pops had everything they needed to make them comfortable, I went downstairs to have my tea and to find out more about our free tickets.

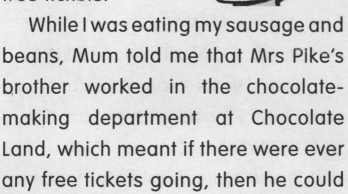

While I was eating my sausage and beans, Mum told me that Mrs Pike's brother worked in the chocolate-making department at Chocolate Land, which meant if there were ever any free tickets going, then he could always get some. Mrs Pike has been to Chocolate Land loads of times for free before, and had decided to give her next free tickets to us. For no money at all!!!

When I asked Mum what day we could go, she said she hadn't decided yet. She said the Spirit of Easter Festival would begin on Good Friday, but it would probably be very busy on the first day.

"GOOD SATURDAY THEN," I begged, "before all the chocolate runs out! Please let's go on GOOD SATURDAY!!!"

"I'll see, Daisy," said Mum, waving

the tickets in the air again. "Let's see if you can be good every day, from Best Ever Friday all the way up to Good Friday, and I'll make a decision then."

"What if I'm not good?" I asked.

"If you're not good, then I will have to choose someone else to go with," said Mum.

Which was another lie.

As soon as I'd finished my toffee yoghurt, I rang Gabby to give her a hamster update AND tell her my latest BEST EVER EVER news.

Gabby told me not to have any breakfast on the day we went to Chocolate Land because you get loads of free chocolate to eat when you arrive there. *And* while you're walking around.

That's the **trouble with breakfast** – it can ruin your appetite.

When I asked Gabby what else there was to do at Chocolate Land, she said there were more things than I could ever dream of. She said there were rides to go on, there was chocolate to eat, there were games to play with, things made of chocolate to see, plus you could even watch actual Chocolate Land chocolate being made! And stirred! And wrapped!!!

When I put the phone down, I almost forgot all about Pickle and Pops. All I could think about was

CHOCOLATE!

"Chocolate Land sounds IMMENSE!" I said to my mum, skidding back into the kitchen.

"All the more reason to behave

yourself this week," said Mum, waving the tickets at me for the THIRD annoying time. "Do you think you can be good, Daisy?" said my mum. "Do you think you can be on your best behaviour for seven whole days in a row?"

Honestly, sometimes you'd think I was always getting into trouble.

CHAPTER 6

Being good all the way up to Good Friday was actually much easier than I thought it would be. In fact, it was really, really easy, because for the first time ever during the Easter holidays I had Pickle and Pops to play with as well as Gabby!

Gabby came round to see me every day. And she brought her pencil case.

"LET'S DO A HAMSTER PROJECT TOGETHER!" she said, the very first morning. "IF WE DO A HAMSTER

PROJECT BASED ON PICKLE AND POPS, WE CAN TAKE IT INTO SCHOOL AND SHOW IT TO EVERYONE IN THE CLASS AFTER EASTER!"

"WE CAN FILL IT WITH LOADS OF FINDINGS!" I said.

Findings are really important if you are going to do a project at home, especially findings you find yourself.

Gabby suggested we call our findings "Furry Findings" because hamsters are furry. We decided we would do "hamsters on the bed" findings, "hamsters on the carpet" findings, and loads of other findings too.

The bag of sawdust that Mrs Pike had given Gabby to carry was so massive it meant I could clean Pickle and Pops out every day. That way I could get proper poo findings.

My three-colour torch had new batteries in, which meant I could get "hamsters in the dark" findings as well.

Gabby had the brilliant idea of getting "twitchiest nose" findings.

I had the idea of getting "hungriest hamster" findings.

Once we had combined our pencils and pens there was no stopping us!

PICKLE AND POPS
Furry Findings
By Daisy Butters and
Gabriella Summers

Pickle - he's a usual hamster.

Pops - he's a Siberian hamster.

Hamster Poo Findings:

(Poo chart)

DAY 1 - 102

DAY 2 - 84

DAY 3 - 93

DAY 4 - 106

DAY 5 - 98

DAY 6 - 89

DAY 7 - 111!

Hamsters on the Bed Findings:

DAY 1 - First one to climb over
my pillow: Pickle

DAY 2 - First one to go under
my covers: Pops

DAY 3 - First one to fall off
my bed: Pops

DAY 4 - First one to chew my
duvet: Pickle

DAY 5 - First one to find a
sunflower seed: Pickle

DAY 6 - First one to poo on my
duvet: Pops

DAY 7 - First one to try
to go back
to sleep: Pickle

Hamsters on the Carpet Findings:

DAY 1 – First one to go behind my wardrobe: Pickle

DAY 2 – First one to poo on the carpet: Pops

DAY 3 – First one to find the blueberry: Pickle

DAY 4 – First one to my bedroom door: Pops

DAY 5 – First one to go under my bed: Pops

DAY 6 – First one to sniff my sock: Pickle

DAY 7 – First one to nibble the carpet: Pickle

In the Dark Findings:

DAY 1 - First one to wake up: Pops

DAY 2 - First one to go on the wheel: Pickle

DAY 3 - First one to sniff my torch: Pops

DAY 4 - First one to poo in the dark: Pickle

DAY 5 - First one to climb cage bars in the dark: Pickle

DAY 6 - First one to blink at my torch: Pops

DAY 7 - First one to fall off my torch: Pickle

Thirstiest Thirst Findings:

DAY 1 - Pickle

DAY 2 - Pops

DAY 3 - Pickle

DAY 4 - Pops

DAY 5 - Pickle

DAY 6 - Pops

DAY 7 - Pops

Twitchiest Nose Findings:

DAY 1 - Pickle

DAY 2 - Pickle

DAY 3 - Pops

DAY 4 - Pickle

DAY 5 - Pops

DAY 6 - Pops

DAY 7 - A draw

Hungriest Hamster Findings:

DAY 1 - Pops

DAY 2 - Pops

DAY 3 - Pops

DAY 4 - Pops

DAY 5 - Pops

DAY 6 - Pops

DAY 7 - Pops

Blinkiest Blink Findings:

DAY 1 - Pops

DAY 2 - Pickle

DAY 3 - Pickle

DAY 4 - Pickle

DAY 5 - Pickle

DAY 6 - Pops

DAY 7 - Pops

By the time Good Friday arrived we had enough furry findings to make a whole TV series about hamsters! Even better, we had something even more exciting to look forward to now. You've guessed it . . .

. . . EASTER EGGS!

CHAPTER 7

The **trouble with Easter eggs** is I only get them at Easter, which means as soon as I'm given them I need to eat one straight away. Or at least a bit of one.

I think most children have to wait till Easter Sunday for their Easter eggs. Gabby has to wait till Easter Sunday, Dylan who lives in my street has to wait until Easter Sunday, and I think most of the children in my class have to wait till Easter Sunday. But I'm not most children. My mum has given up trying to make me wait till Sunday for my Easter eggs because I ask for them too much. Mum says I don't ask, I pester – but I don't pester, I definitely just ask. And ask and ask and ask, until she gives them to me on Good Friday instead.

I always get two Easter eggs at Easter. This year I had a whopping one with chocolate buttons inside it from Mum, and a medium big one with YumYumz in it from Nanny and Grampy.

The **trouble with liking chocolate** is it's really hard to make Easter eggs last.

One year I tried sucking my Easter eggs instead of biting them, but that didn't work.

Another year I tried breaking them up into teensy little pieces and eating each piece with a cocktail stick, but that didn't work either.

It was seventeen minutes past seven when I woke up on Good Friday morning, and only eighteen minutes past seven by the time I

had opened my first egg. My plan this year was to open my biggest egg first. It was so big, I was sure it would have at least four packets of chocolate buttons inside.

Trouble is, when I looked inside the hole, there was only one packet of buttons to open. Which means instead of loads of chocolate buttons I got about eleven.

The **trouble with about eleven chocolate buttons** is they are really easy to eat. So I had to open my YumYumz egg as well.

The **trouble with opening my YumYumz egg** is YumYumz are just as easy to eat as chocolate buttons. Which meant by twenty past seven I'd eaten those as well.

Which meant now I only had four empty halves of Easter egg left!

Except I didn't. Because the **trouble with eating YumYumz straight after chocolate buttons** is it gives me a taste for bigger pieces of Easter egg too, like half a whole YumYumz egg plus a quarter of the other half.

Which meant by half past seven I only had the two halves of my biggest egg left, plus three quarters of my last half of YumYumz egg.

Except the **trouble with three quarters of last halves of any type of Easter egg** is it looks really untidy once you've bitten into it. So I decided to tidy mine up by eating it before breakfast too.

Which meant by twenty-eight minutes to eight I only had the two empty halves of my biggest egg left, AND THERE WERE STILL PRETTY MUCH FOUR DAYS OF EASTER STILL TO GO!

Thank goodness I had a free ticket to Chocolate Land.

By the time I got downstairs for breakfast I didn't really have a taste for Weetabix or Cornflakes or Rice Krispies or Shredded Wheat – or any other kind of breakfast that didn't have chocolate in it.

All I really fancied for breakfast was chocolate. Or at least something that was chocolate flavoured.

Luckily I had some Chocopops in the cupboard.

As soon as Mum sat down to breakfast I asked her if we were definitely going to Chocolate Land on Saturday. I really needed to know because my taste for chocolate had got so big I knew there was no way I could make the last two halves of my second Easter egg last until Easter Monday. Or Easter Sunday. Or even Easter Saturday!

Except the answer Mum gave me wasn't the one I was expecting.

"It's up to you," she said.

The **trouble with Mum saying "It's up to you"** is nothing is ever up to me. So why was she saying it now?

"We can go to Chocolate Land tomorrow, Daisy, but if we do, I'm afraid you will miss the Easter egg hunt that Mrs Pike is having in her garden," she said.

Easter egg hunt? I thought. EASTER EGG HUNT TOMORROW? IN MRS PIKE'S GARDEN?!

"But Mrs Pike never has Easter egg hunts in her garden," I said.

"Well, she is this year," Mum smiled, "and she's inviting all the children in our street."

"But there aren't any children in our street apart from me and Dylan!" I said.

"Of course there are," laughed my mum. "They are just much younger than you. There's Roco and Trixie at number seven, there's Madison at number twenty-two, there's Poppy and Jensen at number seventy-six."

"THEY'RE NOT CHILDREN, THEY'RE BABIES!" I said.

"They are not babies, they are toddlers," said Mum. "And I'm sure they like chocolate just as much as you."

Which isn't possible.

The **trouble with Easter egg hunts on Saturday** is I was desperate to go to Chocolate Land on Saturday.

"What time will the Easter egg hunt be?" I asked.

"Sometime in the afternoon," Mum said.

That was no good. It would take at least three hours just to drive to Chocolate Land. We could never get back to Mrs Pike's in time.

"Why can't she do the Easter egg hunt on Sunday or Monday?" I asked.

"Because she is going to visit her parents on Easter Sunday and Monday," explained Mum.

"But why is Mrs Pike even having an Easter egg hunt if she doesn't have children?"

"Because, Daisy," said Mum, "her brother has sent her a bag of mini chocolate egg seconds from Chocolate Land and she thought it would be a fun thing to do."

The **trouble with fun things to do** is they are no fun at all if you don't do them.

"What's a mini chocolate egg second?" I asked.

"It's a miniature-sized chocolate Easter egg that's not quite perfect enough for Chocolate Land to sell," said Mum.

"What's wrong with it?" I asked.

"It may not be quite the right shape," said Mum. "Or maybe the silver foil it is wrapped in has got a bit torn."

"How mini is mini?" I asked.

"About the size of an acorn, I guess," said Mum.

"But it's still made of chocolate from Chocolate Land?" I asked.

"Yes." Mum nodded.

"All the way through?"

"All the way through." Mum smiled.

Mini egg seconds sounded perfect to me. Trouble is, I really, really, really had a taste for going to Chocolate Land on Saturday, not to Mrs Pike's garden.

"How many mini egg seconds will Mrs Pike be hiding?" I asked.

"I don't know," said Mum.

"How many do you think I will find?" I asked.

"I don't know," said Mum. "It depends how hard you look."

"Why can't she just give the mini egg seconds away instead of forcing children to hunt for them?" I asked. "If she just gave them away, I could have mine now."

"But it wouldn't be an Easter egg

hunt then, would it?" said Mum.

Mum was right, but it didn't make things any easier. I really liked the sound of hunting for mini egg seconds, but I really, really, REALLY liked the sound of going to Chocolate Land instead. So what was it going to be? Chocolate Land on Saturday? Or Easter egg hunt on Saturday?

I was going to have to make one of the most important decisions of my entire life.

CHAPTER 8

The **trouble with making one of the most important decisions of your entire life** is you really need chocolate to help you make it.

By the time Gabby rang my doorbell at nine o'clock I was already halfway through one half of my last two halves of Easter egg.

"You need to help me decide,"

I said to Gabby, racing her up the stairs to my bedroom.

"Decide what?" she said.

"It's really complicated," I told her.

The **trouble with explaining things that are really complicated** is you really need more chocolate to help you do it. Plus, if you are explaining to your best friend, you need to give them half of all the chocolate you have left too. Because that's what best friends forever do.

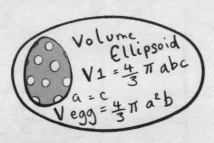

By the time I had explained to Gabby all about Mrs Pike and her mini egg seconds, plus all about the annoying baby children who would be invited to the egg hunt as well, all I had left of my Easter eggs were the wrappers and the boxes.

"If I were you," said Gabby, "I would go to Mrs Pike's on Saturday and find as many mini egg seconds as you can, and then I would go to Chocolate Land on Sunday or Monday and eat all the chocolate you can eat!"

Trouble is, Gabby isn't me. She's Gabby.

The **trouble with Gabby being Gabby** is she'd been to Chocolate Land FOUR times before and I hadn't been there even once.

Which meant it was easy peasy for Gabby to say wait till Sunday or Monday, but really hard for me to even wait until Saturday!

"What if Chocolate Land runs out of chocolate on Saturday?" I asked.

"It won't run out of chocolate," laughed Gabby. "It's CHOCOLATE

LAND! Chocolate Land never runs out of chocolate. It just keeps making it and making it and making it!"

"What if chocolate is banned by the prime minister on Saturday night so that when I arrive at Chocolate Land on Sunday or Monday there's loads of chocolate but no one is allowed to eat it?"

"I think the prime minister would lose his job then," said Gabby.

"What if an alien spaceship comes down out of the sky on Saturday night and beams Chocolate Land up to its own planet?" I asked.

"I hadn't thought of that," Gabby frowned.

The **trouble with not having thought of something** is it makes you want another piece of chocolate.

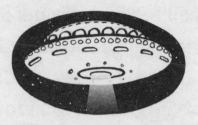

"Have you got any more Easter eggs you can open?" asked Gabby.

"No," I told her. "They're all gone."

The **trouble with Easter eggs being all gone** is it makes you want chocolate even more.

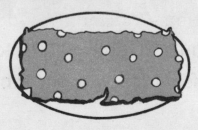

Because after eating two whole Easter eggs, plus all the extra chocolate sweets that are hidden inside, you really, really get the taste.

Gabby had really got the taste too. In fact, from the way she was nearly dribbling I think she might even have got the taste more than me!

"I wish my mum and dad let me have my Easter eggs on Good Friday like your mum does," sighed Gabby. "I could have brought them with me and shared them with you."

"How many do you get?" I asked.

"About six," said Gabby.

The **trouble with finding out that your best friend forever gets SIX Easter eggs** is it makes you get the taste for chocolate even more!

"SIX?" I gasped. "It would take me until lunch time to eat SIX!"

"Once I got nine," said Gabby.

"That's probably more than Mrs Pike will be hiding in her garden tomorrow!" I said. "In fact, in actual chocolate's worth, it's probably loads more, because Mrs Pike's eggs are only mini-sized ones!"

"I don't suppose she could have the Easter egg hunt in her garden today, could she?" asked Gabby. "I could really do with some more chocolate."

"Me too," I said. "But all the babies in the street have been invited tomorrow, not today."

"I'd rather do an Easter egg hunt against babies than children my own age," said Gabby. "If you do go tomorrow, you'll find loads more eggs than the babies will, especially if they're hidden high up."

"I know," I said. "But what if Mrs Pike deliberately hides all the eggs really low down, so only babies can see them?"

"I see what you mean," said Gabby.

"And what if I do find loads more eggs than all the babies?" I said. "What if I do some really good hunting, but then my mum forces me to share all my eggs out at the end? That's exactly the sort of thing my mum would do."

"Babies aren't your best friends forever," said Gabby.

"Exactly," I said.

"So you shouldn't have to share with them," said Gabby.

"Exactly," I said.

"If you share with them, you'll end up all getting the same amount," said Gabby.

"Which is so wrong," I said, "because I'll be the actual one who found them, I'll be the one who's done all the hard hunting work, and they'll be the ones who get to eat them."

"That is so wrong," Gabby frowned.

"Plus," I said, "babies and toddlers have much smaller tummies than adult children like us, which means they only need about one mini egg second to fill themselves up, so what's the point of them finding any eggs in the first place?"

"You are so, so right," said Gabby. "Babies and toddlers shouldn't even be allowed to go on Easter egg hunts. It's a complete waste of chocolate."

"But there's nothing I can do about it," I said, "because it's not my Easter egg hunt. It's Mrs Pike's."

"Do you know what?" said Gabby. "I've completely changed my mind. There is only one place you should be going tomorrow and that is CHOCOLATE LAND!"

"Do you think so?" I asked.

"I know so!" said Gabby.

"THEN CHOCOLATE LAND, HERE I COME!" I cheered.

CHAPTER 9

The **trouble with deciding you are definitely going to Chocolate Land and not to Mrs Pike's baby Easter egg hunt** is it makes you get the taste for chocolate EVEN MORE!

"Do you think we could eat the box?" I said, picking up my YumYumz Easter egg box and sniffing the cardboard.

"I don't think so," said Gabby. "But I'll tell you who would probably love to!"

"WHO?" I said, watching her eyebrows jiggle towards the end of my bed.

"PICKLE AND POPS!" Gabby smiled.

We had been talking about chocolate for so long, I had almost forgotten about Pickle and Pops!

At first I thought Gabby was joking, but as soon as I thought about it I realized that she was absolutely, totally right. If hamsters can eat cardboard loo rolls in my classroom at school, then why can't they eat cardboard Easter egg boxes in my bedroom at home? It was a genius idea!

"Not the silver foil, though," said Gabby as I pulled the inside top cardboard bit out of my YumYumz egg box. "Just the cardboard."

Gabby was right. Giving hamsters silver foil to eat is really dangerous. Especially if they are allergic to metal touched by chocolate.

"Here you go, Pickle! Here you go, Pops!" I said, opening the door of their cage and poking the first piece of YumYumz box inside. "Happy Easter from me and Gabby!"

At first neither of them seemed that interested in our Easter present, but once I'd woken them up with my finger and pushed them out of their bedding, their whiskers started twitching and everything!

"He's eating it!" said Gabby, pressing her face to the bars and watching really closely as Pops began nibbling the cardboard I'd given him. "Give Pickle his own piece too!"

It was such a good idea, I gave them TWO bits of Easter egg box each! In fact, when they both started chewing, I decided to undo the clips at the sides of their cage, lift the roof right off and give them a whole empty Easter egg box each!

"Let's give them a cardboard city to nibble through!" I said, putting the roof back on and then doing up the clips. "The chocolate button box is a skyscraper!"

"And the YumYumz box is a cinema!" laughed Gabby.

Pickle and Pops must have been so pleased with their Easter presents. Not only could they chew them, they could crawl in and out of them, push them around with their noses and even do poos inside them!

It was brilliant! PLUS it took Gabby's and my minds completely off chocolate!

For a while.

It was when we went downstairs to play a trick on Mum that I started thinking about chocolate again.

"PICKLE AND POPS LOVE EASTER EGGS!" I said, walking into the kitchen with Gabby and taking my mum completely by surprise. "THE BIGGER THE EASTER EGGS, THE MORE THEY LIKE THEM!"

The **trouble with playing tricks on my mum** is you shouldn't really do it when she's holding a bag of flour. Especially if the bag is open at the top.

The moment I made her think I'd been feeding Pickle and Pops actual chocolate, she went all stiff and dropped the bag of flour on the floor.

117

The **trouble with dropping a bag of flour on the floor** is it kind of explodes like a big white floury bomb.

"YOU HAVEN'T BEEN FEEDING CHOCOLATE TO PICKLE AND POPS! PLEASE TELL ME YOU HAVEN'T BEEN FEEDING CHOCOLATE TO PICKLE AND POPS! I EXPRESSLY TOLD YOU NOT TO GIVE CHOCOLATE TO THOSE HAMSTERS. IN FACT, I FORBADE YOU FROM GIVING CHOCOLATE TO THOSE

HAMSTERS! PLEASE, PLEASE, PLEASE TELL ME YOU HAVEN'T BEEN FEEDING CHOCOLATE TO PICKLE AND POPS!!!"

"We haven't been feeding chocolate to Pickle and Pops." I grinned. "We've only given them the boxes! TRICKED YOU!"

The **trouble with telling your mum she's been tricked** is, if she's dropped a big floury bomb that covered her shoes and her legs and the kitchen floor and the kitchen cupboard, she might not see the funny side.

In fact, she definitely won't.

Which is why I changed the subject straight away.

"I've decided I want to go to Chocolate Land tomorrow instead of Mrs Pike's Easter egg hunt," I told her.

Trouble is, I wasn't sure if she was listening.

The **trouble with not knowing if someone is listening** is you really need them to go "Yes, Daisy. Good idea, Daisy. We'll go to Chocolate Land tomorrow then, Daisy." But Mum didn't say anything.

Or do anything.

She just stayed stiff.

And sort of starey.

And a bit scary.

The **trouble with Mum going stiff, starey and scary** is I thought she might be dead.

Her eyeballs weren't moving. Even her blinks weren't blinking.

When she finally did move, all she actually did was look down at her feet.

That's when Gabby decided it was time for her to go home.

"Have a great time at Chocolate Land," she whispered, "and thanks

for sharing your Easter egg with me."

Which meant I was going to be left alone with my mum.

"Can I go and play at Gabby's?"

I asked, hoping that Mum still wasn't listening and that I could just run out of the house.

"No you can't," she growled. "You've got some clearing up to do."

CHAPTER 10

The **trouble with having clearing up
to do** is I don't see why I should have
had to do it. I mean, it was *Mum* who
dropped the flour on the floor, not
me.

Good job I did clear it up, though,
because I'm not sure she would have
taken me to Chocolate Land at all if I
hadn't.

Once she had changed her

trousers and swept up all the floury bits I had missed, her stiffness actually began to unstiffen.

"Are you sure you don't want to go to Mrs Pike's Easter egg hunt tomorrow, Daisy?" she said. "I'm baking a Victoria sponge for a picnic in her garden afterwards."

The **trouble with Victoria sponges** is they're not made of chocolate.

"I definitely want to go to Chocolate Land tomorrow," I said.

"There'll be hot cross buns as well," she said.

The **trouble with hot cross buns** is they're not made of chocolate.

"I definitely, definitely want to go to Chocolate Land tomorrow," I said.

"There'll be sandwiches and fizzy drinks," she said.

The **trouble with sandwiches and fizzy drinks** is they're not made of chocolate.

"I thought you said it was up to me," I said.

"It *is* up to you," she said.

"Then I definitely, definitely, definitely want to go to Chocolate Land tomorrow please," I said.

"Definitely?" asked Mum.

"Definitely, DEFINITELY!" I told her.

"Then it's decided," said Mum. "We will be getting up early and going to Chocolate Land tomorrow. BUT before we do, I think the polite thing to do would be to thank Mrs Pike for inviting you to her Easter egg hunt and let her know why you won't be able to come."

The **trouble with polite things to do** is they can be a real nuisance, especially when you don't want to do them.

"Can't *you* tell her?" I asked. "She's *your* friend, not mine."

"Of course she's your friend, Daisy," said Mum. "She wouldn't be inviting you to her Easter egg hunt if she wasn't your friend!"

"What if she gets cross?" I asked.

"Of course she won't get cross," said Mum.

"What if she thinks I like Chocolate Land more than her back garden?" I asked.

"I think most children would like Chocolate Land more than their neighbour's back garden," said Mum.

"What if—"

"No more 'what ifs', Daisy," said Mum. "If you want to go to Chocolate Land tomorrow, then please go and say 'Thank you, but no thank you' to Mrs Pike. And while you're there, thank her for the free tickets she gave us as well."

When I remembered the free tickets, I started to feel much better:

if Mrs Pike hadn't given them to us, we would never have been able to go to Chocolate Land in the first place. Which meant actually, it was Mrs Pike's fault that we weren't going to be going to her own Easter egg hunt!

When we took the sponge cake to give to Mrs Pike, she wasn't cross with me at all. She even gave me a free drink of squash.

"Daisy, I completely understand," she said. "If I were your age, I would much rather go to Chocolate Land than a silly old egg hunt in my back garden. You'll love it at Chocolate Land!"

Which made me feel quite guilty.

"Most of the children coming will be far too young to be of interest to you," she said.

Which made me feel even guiltier.

"I'm just so grateful to your mum for making this lovely cake and for offering to help me make the sandwiches. I have so much to do!"

Which made me feel even guiltier still!

"Is there anything I can do to help?" I said, hoping that there wouldn't be, but thinking I'd better say it anyway.

"Can you blow up balloons?" she asked.

"Not really," I said.

"Can you use an electric knife?"

"No, she can't," interrupted my mum.

"Let me think . . ." said Mrs Pike, buttering the last hot cross bun and then picking up her list of things to do.

"I know exactly what you can do for me, Daisy!" she said, tapping her list with her finger. "You can hide the Easter eggs for the egg hunt!" she said. "Would you like to do that, Daisy? It would save me so much time if you did. Your mum can help me make the sandwiches and you can hide the eggs! What a super idea. I'll go and get them."

The **trouble with someone saying "I'll go and get them"** is it gave me no choice. I had to hide the eggs for the egg hunt whether I liked it or not.

"Here they are!" Mrs Pike said, coming back into the kitchen with the bag of mini egg seconds.

When I saw how many mini egg seconds there were inside the bag, my eyes nearly popped out of my ears. There were ZILLIONS! Well, absolutely LOADS. Plus, they didn't look like mini egg seconds to me.

They looked like mini egg firsts!

There were so many eggs in the bag that if I wasn't quick I'd still be in the garden hiding them when it was time for me to go to bed! I'd be hiding them in the dark! I'd be hiding them with a torch!

And as if that wasn't bad enough, they would all be for babies! Not including Dylan.

What a total waste of eggs, I thought as I carried the bag into Mrs Pike's back garden. *What a total, total waste of chocolate. The sooner I got to Chocolate Land, the better.*

CHAPTER 11

When I woke up on Easter Saturday, my taste for chocolate was immenser than immense. In fact, I'd been dreaming about chocolate all night! I'd dreamed that I owned a new kind of bank, where instead of people paying in real money, they had to pay in chocolate money instead.

It was one of the best dreams I'd ever had – until Jack Beechwhistle turned up and tried to rob the bank. Luckily, when I pushed the chocolate alarm button, a massive gush of runny chocolate gunged down from the ceiling and turned him into a chocolate Jack.

Trouble is, Mum woke me up before I could eat him.

I decided I would take Gabby's advice and completely skip breakfast that morning. Because I needed to leave as much room for chocolate as I could. I didn't tell Mum I was skipping my breakfast because I didn't want her to think she had wasted her time cooking me toast. Or putting jam on it. Instead, I just put it in the bin when she wasn't looking. Mum was really pleased when she saw how quickly my toast had disappeared. And so was I because by half past seven we were on the road!

"What is the Spirit of Easter?" I asked Mum when we got onto the motorway.

"The Spirit of Easter is the true meaning of Easter," she said.

"What's the true meaning of Easter

then?" I asked, not really understanding what she was saying.

"I knew you were going to ask that," said Mum, wriggling her bottom into her seat. "For many people, Daisy, the Spirit of Easter is a special celebration of the time when Jesus came back from the dead. For Chocolate Land, the Spirit of Easter is chocolate."

"Did Jesus like chocolate?" I asked.

"I don't think chocolate was invented when Jesus was around," said Mum. "I don't think there is any mention of chocolate in the Bible at all."

"I was only thinking that maybe if Jesus really, really liked chocolate and was only halfway through a bar when he died, then it would have been a good reason to come back to life again. To finish the bar."

"I think Jesus came back from the dead for much more important reasons than that," said Mum.

"Maybe he had the idea for inventing chocolate and wanted to come back to life so he could tell everyone how to make it."

"I can promise you, Daisy," said Mum, "that chocolate has no part to play in the resurrection of Jesus Christ or anything to do with Christian beliefs."

"So why does Chocolate Land think that the Spirit of Easter is chocolate then?" I asked.

"Because times are changing," said Mum. "More and more people have forgotten what the true meaning of Easter really is."

"So today some people like chocolate more than the Bible?" I asked.

"I guess so," said Mum.

"Did Jesus have pet lambs?" I said.

"You always see pictures of lambs at Easter."

"Jesus was the Lamb of God," said Mum.

"So was Jesus a lamb?"

"No, he wasn't a lamb," sighed my mum.

"Was he woolly?"

"No, he wasn't woolly," said Mum.

"Did he have a woolly coat?"

"No, I don't think so," said Mum.

"But there are lambs in the Bible?"

"Yes, there are definitely lambs in the Bible."

"Is there an Easter Bunny in the Bible?" I asked.

"No, there isn't an Easter Bunny in the Bible," said Mum. "The Easter Bunny is a magical bunny that delivers Easter eggs when you're asleep, but  he has nothing to do with the Bible either."

"A bit like Father Christmas," I said.

"Yes, a bit like Father Christmas, only with longer ears," said Mum.

"Has the Easter Bunny got a sleigh?" I asked.

"No," said Mum.

"So how does he deliver all those eggs?"

"I don't know," said Mum.

"Do his ears help him fly?" I asked.

"Only Dumbo's ears help him fly," said Mum.

"Is Dumbo in the Bible?" I asked.

"No, Dumbo isn't in the Bible," said Mum. "Or Jiminy Cricket, Mickey Mouse, Minnie Mouse, Goofy or Pluto."

"What about little fluffy chicks?"

I asked. "You always see little fluffy yellow chicks at Easter."

"That's because they are born around Easter time," said Mum. "They have nothing to do with Jesus or the Bible. They are just born around Easter time. Easter time is spring time too, Daisy. Lots of animals are born in the spring time."

"I bet Jesus liked fluffy yellow chicks best," I said.

"Everyone likes fluffy yellow chicks best," said my mum, "but they have nothing to do with the Bible."

"Are there any big, fully-grown chickens in the Bible?" I asked.

"I'm not sure," said Mum.

"Are there any tiger cubs in the Bible?" I asked.

"Are there any dinosaurs in the Bible?" I asked.

"In a race, who do you think would win out of Jesus, Santa and the Easter Bunny?" I asked.

"If you were a chocolate bar, which chocolate bar would you want to be?"

"If you were an egg, which kind of chick would you want to hatch into?"

I think Mum was really pleased to get to Chocolate Land.

CHAPTER 12

I knew we had arrived at Chocolate Land the instant we got to Chocolate Land because there was a huge sign above the entrance to Chocolate Land that said 'CHOCOLATE LAND'.

The **trouble with being totally sure I'd arrived at Chocolate Land** is it made my taste buds go all chocolaty straight away.

When I wound my window down and smelled the chocolate, even my eyeballs turned chocolaty!

The Chocolate Land building was immense. It looked like a massive great football made out of chocolate squares.

"Hurry up and park!" I shouted at my mum. "Quick! Before all the chocolate runs out!"

The **trouble with hurrying up and parking** is you can't do it at Chocolate Land because there are so many cars in the queue.

Toffee parking zone was full, *Fruit and Nut* parking zone was full, *Half Milk* was full, *Full Milk* was full, *Truffle* parking zone wasn't actually full, but someone had parked across two spaces.

"Remember *Caramel* zone, row fifty-six," said my mum as we finally,

finally, finally managed to find a space.

"I told you it would be busy," Mum said as she locked the car. "OK, Daisy, LET'S DO THIS!"

The **trouble with doing Chocolate Land** is you can't just do it.

The SPIRIT of EASTER

Because first you have to stand in a queue for ages too.

"Look at all the people," I groaned. "What if they eat all the chocolate before we get inside?!!!"

Luckily there was chocolate to eat outside the building too.

As soon I saw the Easter Bunny giving away free chocolates, there was no way I was staying in the queue.

The **trouble with seeing the Easter Bunny giving away free chocolates** is you have to jump on him straight away.

Otherwise he might forget to give you some.

And guess what? They weren't even ordinary chocolates either. They were actual mini egg firsts! Well, they were until the Easter Bunny dropped them.

Mum said he didn't drop them, I made him drop them, plus jumping on the back of the Easter Bunny isn't a very polite thing to do.

I still got nine free mini eggs though. Plus I got to give him a really big hug. And stroke his ears. You should have felt how fluffy they were! You should have heard him squeak!

After Mum had helped him stand up again, she made me say sorry and told me to go back to the queue. Which was a bit of a shame really, because there were still lots of free eggs I hadn't had a chance to pick up.

Luckily, there were loads of other children nearby to help grab all the ones I'd missed. In fact, thanks to us, the Easter Bunny didn't have to put one single free chocolate mini egg back into his basket!

Picking up nine chocolate mini egg firsts was actually really handy because it gave me something to eat while we were standing in the queue.

Standing in a queue is a hundred times easier when you're eating chocolate. Especially free chocolate. In fact, if I'd been able to grab about hundred more of those eggs, I reckon I could have queued for about another ten hours. Maybe even eleven. Maybe even eleven and three quarters.

I don't think Mum could have, though. By the time we got right up close to the entrance, she was saying things that weren't the spirit of Easter at all.

They certainly weren't things that you would hear in the Bible.

"TEN . . .

NINE . . .

EIGHT. . ." I said, counting the number of people that were still ahead of us in the queue.

"SEVEN,

SIX,

FIVE . . ." I smiled as Mum opened her handbag and took out our free tickets.

"FOUR,

THREE,

TWO,

ONE . . ."

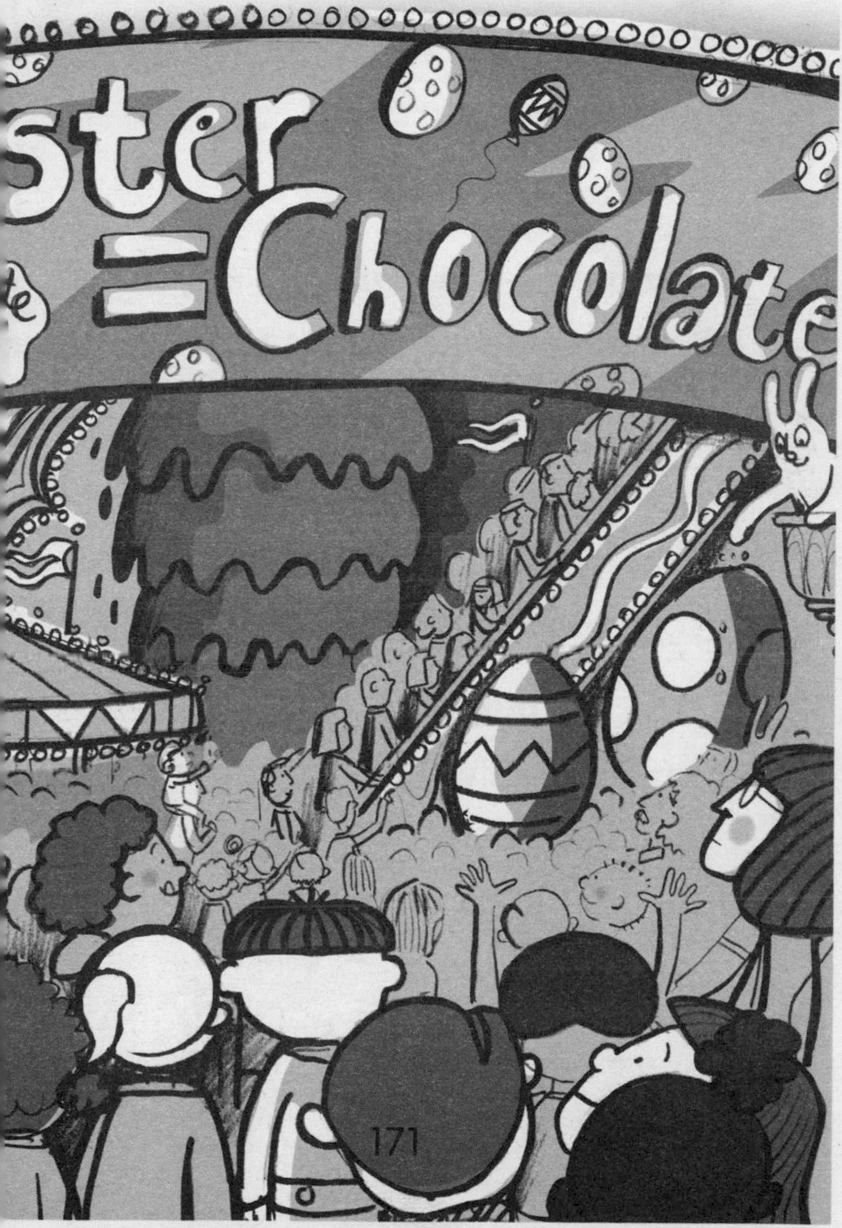

ster
=Chocolate

CHAPTER 13

As soon as we were in, my mum bought a special map that showed us all the places we could go.

The **trouble with special maps** is they are really hard to understand, especially when there are so many different things to look at.

"Let's go this way," said Mum,
pushing me through the crowds
of people in the direction of the
chocolate rock climbing.

The **trouble with chocolate rock climbing** is I'd never climbed a giant chocolate rock before, especially a chocolate rock made of plastic to make it look like a giant chocolate bar.

Chocolate rock climbing is one of the most dangerous things you can do. You have to wear special ropes and a special helmet and everything. Even better, if you climb to the top, guess what you win? A chocolate bar!

The **trouble with winning a chocolate bar** is once you've eaten it, it gives you the taste for more chocolate. So I asked Mum if I could write my name on an Easter egg next.

The **trouble with writing your name on an Easter egg** is there are only five letters in DAISY, which means you don't get very much writing on your egg.

When the lady asked me what my name was, I told her it was Cinderella Thumbelina Butters because I thought she might give me a bigger egg to write on. Trouble is, all the eggs were the same size.

So I underlined my name seven times.

The **trouble with eating an Easter egg underlined seven times** is it gives you the taste for more chocolate AND more icing too!

So we went to do face painting next.

Face painting at Chocolate Land is better than any type of face painting I've ever done.

The **trouble with normal face painting** is they use paint, but at Chocolate Land they do it with warm, runny chocolate! PLUS they use icing to do the whiskers!

Not only that – they don't let you see your face until the warm, runny chocolate has gone cold!

The **trouble with warm, runny chocolate that's gone cold** is that as soon as you laugh, it cracks!

And as soon as it cracks, you have to eat it! It was brilliant!!!!

After we'd done chocolate face painting, Mum said she needed a sit-down. So we went to watch a Chocolate Land rock concert.

The **trouble with Chocolate Land rock concerts** is you really need to get there early, because that way you can stand at the front, because once the rock people have finished playing their chocolate instruments, they smash them all up and you get to eat those too!

Trouble is, we got there quite late so we had to sit at the back. Which meant I didn't even get a piece of chocolate guitar string.

The **trouble with not even getting a piece of chocolate guitar string** is it makes you get the taste for chocolate even more, so we went to do a Chocolate Land jigsaw.

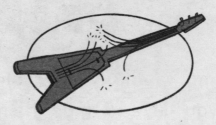

Chocolate Land jigsaws are much better than ordinary jigsaws because they are already done. So instead

of putting them together piece by piece, you have to undo them piece by piece and eat the pieces while you are undoing them.

Mum said she liked the edge

pieces best, but I liked the pieces with the curly bits.

After we'd eaten a chocolate jigsaw, I asked Mum if we could go to the chocolate fountain. I'd heard of chocolate fountains but I'd never actually dipped anything in one.

When we got there, there was a really long queue, but it was all right because I'd taken some extra jigsaw pieces to eat while we were waiting.

The **trouble with extra jigsaw pieces** is, if you hold them in your hand for too long they start to melt, so I had to eat them really quickly. Which was a good job actually, because while we were standing in the queue for the chocolate fountain a man came along and gave everyone a bag of marshmallows!

At first, I didn't know what was in my bag because I'd never had marshmallows before, but when I tried them, I really liked them.

The **trouble with really liking marshmallows** is that by the time we got to the front of the queue, all my marshmallows had gone. So Mum gave me her bag to dip instead.

Dipping marshmallows in a giant chocolate fountain is the best! Especially in a chocolate fountain that changes flavour all the time. It was so brilliant – when the music changed, the chocolate in the

chocolate fountain changed too! Sometimes it was brown chocolate, sometimes it went to white chocolate and other times it was dark brown chocolate. (My marshmallows stayed the same colour all the time. Apart from once I'd dipped them.)

Once my marshmallows had all been dipped, Mum said she needed another sit-down, so we went to see the chocolate dolphin show.

The **trouble with chocolate dolphins** is they can't do the same tricks as normal dolphins.

All they can do is swim round and round in chocolate. Which gets a bit boring after a while.

So we went to the Chocolate Land magic show instead.

Chocolate Land's magic show is amazing because it has a magician in it with a chocolate magic wand! He pulled a chocolate Easter Bunny out of a hat, he sawed a chocolate lady in half and then joined her back together again, he got a chocolate Easter egg to float in the air above his hanky, he did chocolate card tricks and chocolate juggling tricks and chocolate disappearing tricks,

but the best bit was right at the very end of the show, when he kept finding white chocolate doves in the newspaper he was reading!

It was so funny, because every time he threw a dove up into the air to let it go, it just fell back down onto the stage and broke into lots of chocolaty pieces.

That's the **trouble with white chocolate doves**. They CAN'T FLY!

Which meant every time they

crash-landed, children at the front of the audience could climb up onto the stage, grab the pieces and eat them!

And guess double what? This time I was sitting at the front!

It was AWESOME! In fact, if my mum hadn't told me there was somewhere else we needed to be, I could probably have stayed eating white chocolate dove pieces for the rest of the entire day!!!

But we had to go.

"Come on, young lady," Mum said, lifting me down from the stage. "There's somewhere we need to be."

"Where do we need to be?" I asked.

"It's a surprise, Daisy," she said with a smile. "It's a very chocolaty surprise!"

CHAPTER 14

The **trouble with very chocolaty surprises** is everything at Chocolate Land is a chocolaty surprise.

The man on chocolate stilts was a surprise, the chocolate ball pool was a surprise, the chocolate stunt show was a surprise, the chocolate planetarium was a surprise, the chocolate ping pong was a surprise. Everything was a surprise – except every time we reached a new chocolaty surprise, Mum kept pulling me past it!

When I saw the massive queue for the Chocolate Land Wrapperama Experience, I did everything I could to pull her in that direction, but the harder I pulled, the harder she tugged me the other way.

"We need to be somewhere very special at three o'clock, Daisy," she said, "and it's five to three now!"

"But I want to be wrapped up in silver foil like a chocolate bar! All the other children are doing it!"

"We'll get you wrapped up like a chocolate bar afterwards," she promised.

The **trouble with trying to get somewhere very special fast** is it's really difficult at Chocolate Land because there are so many people in the way.

I didn't know where Mum was taking me, but we walked and walked and walked. At the top of the escalator she even asked me to shut my eyes!

If my arms had been made of chewing gum, then I reckon they would have stretched to about a

kilometre long by the time Mum actually stopped me and went,

"TA-DAH!"

The **trouble with someone going "TA-DAH!"** is you can't always tell why they are ta-dahing. Especially if your eyes are closed.

"Now you know why Chocolate Land never runs out of chocolate, Daisy!" she said.

"LOOK!"

When I opened my eyes and looked down, I saw we were really high up on a great big, long platform, looking down on the actual place where actual Chocolate Land chocolates are actually made!

There were shiny machines doing all kinds of different chocolaty things. There was a great, big circle of runny chocolate. There were lots of different people doing different chocolaty jobs. It was the best TA-DAH EVER!

"SURPRISE, DAISY!" said Mum, putting her hands on both of my shoulders and then making me face the other way.

"Hello, Daisy," said a man I'd never met before. "My name's David. I'm Mrs Pike's brother. Would you like to come and help me stir the chocolate?"

The **trouble with talking to strangers called David** is it made me go a bit shy at first.

"I'll be coming too," whispered Mum.

As soon as I realized Mum was coming with me I knew exactly what to say to David.

"YES, PLEASE!"

Can you believe it? I was actually going to get to stir Chocolate Land's actual chocolate!!!! All by myself! With my mum.

The **trouble with stirring actual chocolate at actual Chocolate Land all by yourself with your mum** is you can't just go and do it.

You have to go with David through some secret doors, down in a lift, through some more secret doors and into a special room that only Chocolate Land people are allowed into. Not only that. You then have to put on special clothes that only Chocolate Land people are allowed to wear too.

I had to put plastic bags over my shoes. I had to wear a white coat, some rubber gloves, a plastic hat and even a mask like doctors wear on the telly. It was so exciting.

There was a special changing room for my mum and a special changing room for me next door. When we came out, we both saw each other wearing Chocolate Land

clothes for the very first time. Mum looked so funny!

Once we'd stopped giggling, David told us that when we went through the next door, we would be stepping into the actual Chocolate Land factory where all the chocolate is made.

He told us that a few words would be said about the Spirit of Easter Festival, and then I – yes, me, Daisy Butters and no one else – would be invited to stir the Chocolate Land chocolate with a special Chocolate Land spoon!

"Time to go!" said David, opening the next secret door.

Stepping out into the factory was totally weird. Instead of being up, looking down, now I was down, looking up! There were hundreds of people lined up all the way along the platform above me, and they were all looking at me.

When I saw the spoon, I nearly fell over! It was the size of a canoe paddle!

All I had to do was wait for the few words to be over, and then I could get stirring with my Spirit of Easter spoon!

"Welcome, ladies, gentlemen and ESPECIALLY children, to the Chocolate Land Spirit of Easter Festival! Easter, as you know, is a time for chocolate, a time for people of all cultures and all faiths to buy chocolate, to eat chocolate and to share chocolate. It is a time to reflect on the many precious moments when chocolate has added real meaning to our lives; when it has comforted us, nourished us, protected us and sustained us, day after day after day.

"Chocolate Land is proud to be the biggest manufacturer of chocolate confectionery in the country. We *pride ourselves not only on the quality of the chocolates we produce, but also on the exceptionally high standards of hygiene that we bring to the manufacturing process.*

"You are looking at a canal of pure molten chocolate, two metres deep and four metres wide and stretching half a kilometre in length. Four million litres of Chocolate Land chocolate flow through our confectionery canal at any one time. All the more chocolate eggs for Easter!"

It sounded like a lot more than a few words to me, but luckily there were only a few more to go.

"Now then, once a day, every day during our Easter Festival, we like to bring something a little extra special to our Easter chocolate. Ladies and gentlemen, will you please welcome today's special guest, Miss Daisy Butters! If you'd like to climb the steps, Daisy, then the Spirit of Easter Chocolate Stirring Ceremony can commence."

When I looked up at all the people who were looking down at me, I saw they weren't just looking at me, they were clapping me! Even the children were clapping me! Really big claps, too!

The steps up to the Chocolate Stirring looked really easy to climb, but as I walked towards them, two ladies in Chocolate Land clothes came to help me. One took my spoon and the other took my hand. Which was a bit annoying really, because I didn't need anyone's help at all. In fact, I could probably have climbed right up to the edge of the chocolate canal without even using the steps.

As soon as I got to the top, I turned to look at my mum. She was giving me two big rubber thumbs-up now. She was so proud! I was so excited!

If only the lady standing next to me hadn't suddenly shouted:

CHAPTER 15

The **trouble with someone shouting "RAT!" really, really loudly in Chocolate Land** is not only did it make me drop the spoon, it made everyone in Chocolate Land think there was an actual rat near the Chocolate Land chocolate – when ACTUALLY there wasn't a rat near the chocolate at all. There was a hamster.

The instant I spotted Pops running right along the edge of the chocolate canal, I shoved my hands into my pockets to check that Pickle was still there.

Trouble is, when I grabbed him, I squeezed him too hard.

The **trouble with squeezing hamsters too hard** is that it isn't just their eyes that can pop out – sometimes their teeth can pop out too. I think that's why he bit me.

The **trouble with being bitten by a hamster** is it really made me jump.

Which meant instead of putting

him back in my pocket, I kind of flung him through the air.

The **trouble with flinging a hamster through the air** is that if you do it in the Chocolate Land factory when you are standing right beside the chocolate, there are only two places he can land: on the floor or in the chocolate.

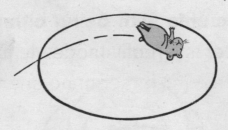

As soon as I saw Pickle flying through the air towards the chocolate, I suddenly remembered everything

Mum had told me about chocolate being the worst thing you could ever give a hamster to eat, let alone swim in!

Which is why, as soon as he landed in the chocolate, I shouted,

"PICKKKKKKLE!"

The **trouble with shouting "Pickle!" in Chocolate Land** is Chocolate Land doesn't make pickle. It makes chocolate. Which meant no one knew what I meant.

Oops!

So I had to shout,

"MY HAMSTER!"

instead.

I think that was the moment when Mum realized what I had done. She didn't say anything – she just went stiffer than I'd ever seen her go before.

The **trouble with Mum going stiffer than I'd ever seen her go before** is it meant I had to do all the chasing.

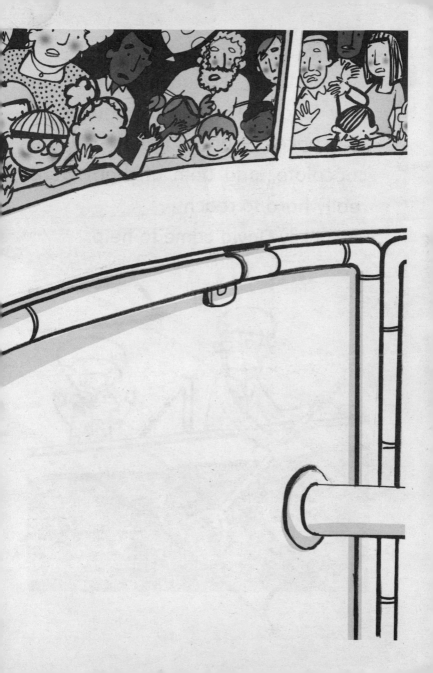

Trouble is, I didn't know which way to chase. I had a hamster *by* the chocolate and a hamster *in* the chocolate, and both of them were really hard to reach.

Luckily David came to help.

It took him about five goes to lift Pickle out of the chocolate with the spoon. And it took me about eight grabs to get Pops back into my pocket. Boy, was I pleased to get them both back!

And, boy, was everyone pleased to find out that there weren't any rats near the chocolate, only hamsters! At least, I think they were pleased. It was a bit hard to tell.

Luckily Pops hadn't fallen into the chocolate like Pickle had, but unfortunately some of his poos kind of might have. No one was exactly sure how many poos he'd done, but there were definitely some on the edge of the canal where he had been running. He must have been really excited because I counted

seventeen!

The **trouble with hamster poos falling into chocolate or even being near chocolate** is it's actually quite serious. At least, David said it was. It's all right if peanuts fall into chocolate or raisins fall into chocolate, but if it's hamster poos or even whole hamsters, all the chocolate has to be thrown away.

And all the chocolate-making machines have to be turned off and cleaned.

Don't ask me why, because hamster germs must be absolutely teensy weensy.

But David said it was the law.

I had a bit of a bad feeling after that.

I think everyone looking down from the platform did too. Because none of them were clapping me any more. All  they were doing was pointing and gasping.

When we came out of the changing rooms with our normal

 clothes back on again, even my mum's ears looked stiff. David's face looked a teensy bit cross too.

The **trouble with throwing away four million litres of chocolate** is, for the first time in chocolate history, Chocolate Land was about to run out of chocolate. Plus they would have to spend the next two days cleaning all their chocolate-making machines.

Which meant they would have to close on Easter Sunday and Easter Monday.

Which meant their Spirit of Easter Festival was kind of over.

Thank goodness I had got there before it happened!

CHAPTER 16

"HAMSTERS? TO CHOCOLATE LAND, DAISY?" groaned my mum as we got back into the lift. "HOW COULD YOU EVEN THINK OF TAKING HAMSTERS INTO CHOCOLATE LAND!!??"

The **trouble with taking hamsters into Chocolate Land** is I don't think hamsters are actually allowed.

You'd never know they weren't

allowed because when you walk in through the front doors, all it says is NO DOGS ALLOWED. It doesn't say anything about hamsters at all. Which isn't my fault either.

I thought going to Chocolate Land would be a really nice day out for Pickle and Pops, especially if they stayed asleep in my pockets all day. Trouble is, when I got changed into my Chocolate Land clothes and switched them from my anorak pockets to the pockets of my white coat, I think I must have woken them up. Which isn't my fault either. Because it wasn't even my idea to put Chocolate Land clothes on in the first place. It was David's!

Trouble is, Mum said EVERYTHING was my fault.

When I offered to eat the four million litres of chocolate that

Chocolate Land was having to throw away, she gave me the stiffest look ever.

When I asked if we could go on the Wrapperama Experience and get wrapped up like a chocolate bar next, she just led me out of the building and made me walk back to *Caramel* zone row fifty-six.

Mum said the only thing I would be wrapping myself in now was a duvet when I got home. Which was so unfair!

We didn't talk about the Spirit of Easter again after that. In fact, Mum didn't talk to me all the way home.

Which was kind of handy really because it gave me time to pick the chocolate out of Pickle's fur.

It was gone 5:45 by the time I got Pickle back to normal, and seven by the time we got back to our house. Trouble is, my mum wasn't back to normal at all. She was still really cross.

The **trouble with my mum still being really cross** is Mrs Pike looked a bit crossish too.

When I saw her face looking out of her lounge window at us, I suddenly felt really, really tired. So as soon as my mum opened the front door, I ran straight up to my bedroom with Pickle and Pops, because I was sure they would be really tired too. Trouble is, before Mum had a chance to close our front door, Mrs Pike came over to talk to her.

The **trouble with Mrs Pike talking to Mum** is it made Mum decide to start talking to me again.

Even though I was really, really, really tired now and already fast asleep under my duvet.

"I've just been talking to Mrs Pike," Mum said, totally waking me up. "She's had a lovely conversation with her brother on the phone. She's so thrilled you had such a lovely time at Chocolate Land with Pickle and Pops, Daisy. She's also a little bit puzzled by the Easter egg hunt she had in her garden this afternoon. Apparently none of the children could find any eggs. They hunted high and they hunted low, but the toddlers couldn't find any eggs, their parents couldn't find any eggs, Mrs Pike couldn't find any eggs, even Dylan couldn't find any eggs. So tell me, Daisy, when Mrs Pike and I were in her kitchen making cakes and sandwiches, where exactly did you hide the eggs?"

When Mum found out I'd hidden Mrs Pike's mini egg seconds under my bed, she went as stiff as the stiffest thing you could ever think of with added stiffeners in it.

She made me take all fifty eggs out from under my bed, count them, share them out and then deliver them to all the babies in the street. And Dylan. It was so embarrassing.

Then I had to go and say sorry to Mrs Pike.

Then I had to write a sorry letter to David and the Chocolate Land people.

Then I had to clean my teeth three times.

And then I had to go to bed with no supper, even though all the chocolate and marshmallows I had eaten at Chocolate Land had completely gone down and I was hungry again.

Honestly, it was so unfair. Pickle and Pops were allowed to have something to eat. Mum filled up their food bowl, PLUS gave them some blueberries, PLUS filled up their water bottle too! Even though what happened at Chocolate Land was TOTALLY THEIR FAULT!

Luckily, I'd hidden fifty more mini egg seconds in my slippers.

P.S. Everyone at school loved our furry findings!

DAISY'S
TROUBLE INDEX

The trouble with . . .

Have you read Daisy's other stories?

DAISY
and the TROUBLE with
VAMPIRES

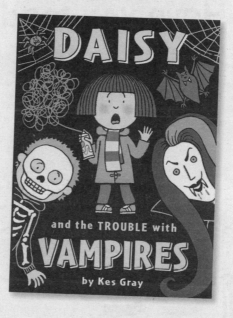

It's Halloween and Daisy is going trick-or-treating for the very first time. In the dark . . . in the fog . . . with a VAMPIRE . . . armed only with a torch and some silly string.

GULP!

DAISY

and the TROUBLE with

LIFE

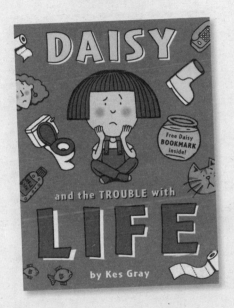

It's SOOOOOOOOOOOOOOOO unfair.

Daisy's been grounded. No HOPPING or SKIPPING, FLYING or PARACHUTING.

She's lucky she's even been allowed out

of her bedroom after what she's done.

But what HAS she done that is SOOOOOOOOOOOOOOOO naughty?

www.daisyclub.co.uk

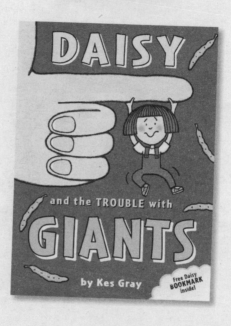

DAISY
and the TROUBLE with
ZOOS

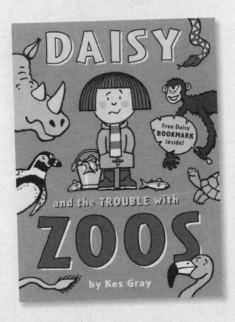

Daisy loves surprises! Especially special birthday surprises – like a trip to the ZOO!!! Who'd have guessed a rhino could do so much wee all in one go! Who'd have imagined an elephant tooth was that heavy! TROUBLE is, the biggest surprise is yet to come.

DAISY
and the TROUBLE with
KITTENS

Daisy is going on holiday! In an actual plane to actual Spain!
It's so exciting! She's never seen a palm tree before, or eaten octopus,
or played Zombie Mermaids, or made so many new friends!
TROUBLE is, five of them are small and cute and furry!

www.daisyclub.co.uk

DAISY
and the TROUBLE with
COCONUTS

Whoooppee!!! The funfair has come to town and Daisy's nanny and grampy are going to take her. Daisy has never been to a funfair before! She can't wait to go on all the rides and play all the games, but she is even more determined to win her very first actual coconut. Trouble is, just how easy will it be to win one?

DAISY
and the TROUBLE with
CHRISTMAS

It's Christmas and Daisy has been given an actual part in the actual school Christmas play! She has special lines to learn and even a special costume to wear!! Trouble is . . . there's something about baby Jesus that isn't quite special enough . . .

DAISY
and the TROUBLE with
PIGGYBANKS

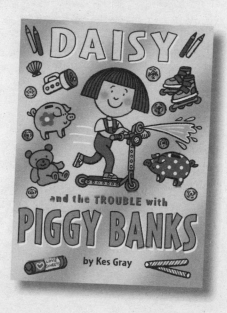

When Daisy's best friend Gabby gets the most awesome, immense, water-squirting micro-scooter Daisy's ever seen, Daisy knows she's got to have one too! Trouble is, they cost a LOT of money. So Daisy and Gabby hatch a money-making plan – what could possibly go wrong?

DAISY

and the TROUBLE with

SPORTS DAY

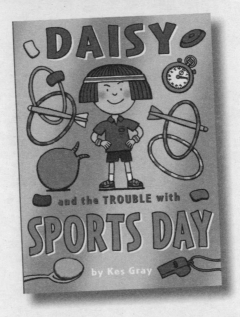

Daisy's determined to win her Sports Day race, and she and best friend Gabby are training hard. They're going for gold! They're in the zone! They're sticking to a strict athlete's diet of Mars bars, Twiglets and cheese strings! Trouble is, everyone else in the class wants to win too . . .

JACK BEECHWHISTLE

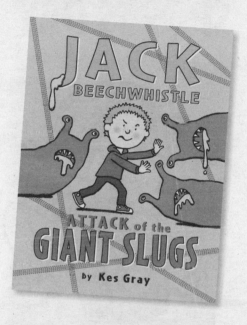

Have you read Jack's daring adventure?

Jack Beechwhistle is here to protect the world from alien attacks, zombie sweet-shop owners, and exploding conkers. His missions are always dangerous and deadly, but Jack's about to face his most challenging test yet: **The Attack of the Giant Slugs**.